BACK TO THE KLONDIKE

First published in the United States
of America in 1989 by The Mallard Press

Mallard Press and its accompanying design
and logo are trademarks of BDD Promotional
Book Company, Inc.

Produced by
Twin Books
15 Sherwood Place
Greenwich, CT 06830

ISBN 0-792-45237-2

Printed in Hong Kong

Twin Books

MALLARD
PRESS

"Why are you cutting out those hearts?" asked Scrooge McDuck.

"For Valentine's Day," said Webby. "Haven't you ever received one?"

"Who would give me one of those?" grunted Scrooge, going into his study. Later, Webby and Scrooge's nephews found him there, staring at a silk heart.

"Ooh, who gave you that, Unca Scrooge?" asked Webby.

"Long ago," began Scrooge, "I went looking for gold in the Klondike. On Saturdays, I'd go to town for supplies, and I'd stop at Dangerous Dan's Honky-Tonk Saloon."

"That sounds like the Old West," said Huey.
"It was," said Scrooge. "Canada was full of gold-seekers, adventurers, gamblers, robbers—and saloons like Dangerous Dan's. That's where I met Glittering Goldie."
"She gave you the silk heart, I bet!" said Webby.

Scrooge continued. "Dan ordered Goldie to invite me to a card game. All was well, at first. I was winning. Then, Goldie switched the cards on me, and I lost."

"That's cheating!" said Huey.

"Yes!" said Scrooge. "And I told them to give me back me money."

"Wow!" said Webby. "Just like in the movies!"

"Well, Dangerous Dan and I had the biggest fight in Klondike history. He was twice me size, and everyone bet that Dan would win. But he didn't! He landed in the river, and didn't set foot in the Honky-Tonk until I was long gone."

"And Goldie?" asked Webby anxiously.

"Well, I was pretty angry. I liked Goldie, but she had tricked me, and I told her I was going to call the Mounted Police."

"Well, you had no choice," said Louie.

"But she begged me to forgive her. She said she'd return every cent if I would just give her a job in me gold mine."

"And you refused, right?"

"No!" replied Scrooge. "I accepted gladly."

"You didn't let her work for free!" cried Webby.
"I was going to share all the gold with her," replied Scrooge. "I wanted to get her out of that saloon. That winter, Goldie and I mined a nice pile of gold. I thought she was wonderful!"

"One day Goldie gave me a valentine—this silk heart. I was the happiest duck in the world!" said Scrooge.

"How romantic!" sighed Webby.

"I asked her then and there to marry me," Scrooge continued. "She agreed, and went off to town to get some things we needed. I was to meet her there the next day.

"The next morning, all the gold we had mined together had disappeared."

"Oh no!" groaned Webby.

"I went looking for Goldie to tell her," said Scrooge, "but Dan said she'd left town to start a new life."

"What a shame!" sighed Huey.

"I worked at the mine until I had another ton of gold, and then I came home. That's the whole story."

"Did you ever go back?" asked Dewey.

"No," replied Scrooge. "The place holds sad memories for me."

"I'd love to see it!" said Louie.

"I suppose we could all go together," said Scrooge.

"Great!" said the nephews, and the very next day, they set off.

Scrooge's old cabin was still there, and someone was living in it. The door opened and there stood Goldie, pointing a pistol at them. "What do you want, strangers?" she demanded.

"Goldie, it's me!" said Scrooge, excited.

"Well, Scrooge McDuck. So, you finally came back."

"That's a fine greeting!" said Scrooge. "You know I only went away to forget."

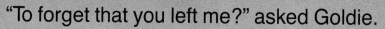

"To forget that you left me?" asked Goldie.

"It was *you* who left *me*, and took the gold."

Goldie pulled the trigger. The bullet missed Scrooge and broke off a piece of rock behind him. Something gleamed underneath.

"*Gold*! You've found a new vein!" exclaimed Scrooge.

"It's all yours," said Goldie. Then she whistled, and a bear appeared. She climbed on his back and rode into the woods.

Before long, Scrooge and his nephews had mined a ton of gold. Dangerous Dan and his buddy watched from behind a rock. "We'll move in when they've got all of it," said Dan.

A few days later, Scrooge and the lads loaded their sacks of gold on the train to head home.

Just as they were about to pull out, Dangerous Dan stopped the train.

"We'll take that gold, Scrooge," said Dan.

"Don't be stupid," said Scrooge. "I'll beat you again, like I did all those years ago!"

"You paid for that, Scrooge!" Dan gloated. "Goldie didn't steal your gold. I did!"

"You told me she'd left town with it."

"She didn't,"said Dan. "You see, I told her *you* had left with all the gold!"

"You...you villain! I'll—"

Dan was about to raise his gun when suddenly Goldie came riding up on her bear, shooting furiously.

Dan and his henchman ran away.
"Are you boys okay?" asked Goldie.
"Never better," said Scrooge. "Goldie, I want to tell you what Dan just told me."

That night, Scrooge and Goldie sat together in the moonlight, remembering old times.

"Are you sure you won't come back with me?"

"No, Scrooge. I belong here now. We had our time."

Scrooge sighed. Sadly, he watched a steam engine puff across the valley below. The smoke rose up into the air, forming a perfect heart.

SUPERDOO!

"Come on, Woodchucks!" called Launchpad McQuack. "Let's get to the camp by dark!"

The Junior Woodchucks were on a campout, and Launchpad had offered to be their leader.

Huey stopped to wait for Launchpad's sidekick, Doofus, to catch up.

"This pack weighs a ton!" puffed Doofus. He was very chubby, and very clumsy, but everyone liked him.

"At last!" gasped Doofus, dropping to the ground when they arrived at the campsite.

"You can rest later," said Launchpad. "First, go find some firewood while the rest of us raise the tents."

"Yessir!" said Doofus, racing off.

A while later, the campers heard a scream. It was Doofus, trying to balance himself on a log that was rolling down the hill, heading straight for the camp. In seconds, all the tents were knocked to the ground.

"You're a walking disaster!" said one of the boys. "Now we'll have to sleep outdoors!"

"I'm awfully sorry," mumbled Doofus. "I just slipped."

"It's okay," said Dewey. "Let's just clear up this mess."

At that very moment, two strange creatures were piloting their spaceship through outer space.

"I think we've lost Star Police," said one.

"Yes, Bobox, but we'd better hide the stone until we're sure they're no longer after us. There's a good place," he said, heading for Earth.

"Just think, Feox. The energy crystal! We'll rule the world!" He opened the window and flung the crystal to Earth.

The next morning, the Woodchucks were up early.

"Today," said Launchpad, "we'll try to find new rocks for our collection. Whoever finds the oddest sample wins a medal."

"Gee, I'd like to win," thought Doofus wistfully. He never saw the piece of metal sticking up out of the ground until he tripped over it. He took the crystal out of the metal box and ran to show it to Launchpad.

Launchpad couldn't find the stone in his handbook, but Doofus decided to keep the stone anyway, and hung it around his neck on a cord.

By mid-afternoon, the Woodchucks had reached a camp by the lake. They played games for a while, then went to bed in warm wooden huts. A stream of moonlight shone on the crystal around Doofus' neck. Suddenly, the stone flashed and Doofus, still fast asleep, floated out the window.

43

The cold air woke him. "What? What am I doing up here?" he screamed, frightened.

Suddenly, he bumped into a boulder. The boulder split in half, but Doofus didn't feel a thing. He picked up a heavy piece of the rock, and it seemed light as a feather!

"My crystal must be magic!" he said, amazed. "No one can say I'm clumsy anymore. Now I'm Superdoofus." He thought for a moment. "No, I'm Superdoo! They'll never know it's because of the crystal."

The Junior Woodchucks had all sorts of contests planned for that week. Doofus surprised them by winning everything. Nobody could beat him at making pancakes, canoeing, or tying knots. Launchpad and the others were puzzled by this sudden change.

"Congratulations, Doofus," said Launchpad. "That's your fifth badge. One more and you'll be Junior Woodchuck of the Year!"

By now, the spacemen had landed on Earth and found the metal box empty. They followed Doofus' tracks to camp.

Feox glanced at the wooden huts and said, "We can destroy those with one shot from our lasers."

Bobox carried something strange over his shoulder. He pointed it at the camp and fired. Luckily, he was holding it backward. The woods caught fire instead of the camp.

The spacemen ran off just as the camp alarm rang out.
"The woods are on fire!" cried Launchpad.
"I must do something," thought Doofus. "But if they find out about the crystal, I'll never be Junior Woodchuck of the Year. Unless..."
He ran to his hut, locked the door, then dug through his pack. Moments later, he came out in long pants, boots, a mask, and a cape. He flew off toward the fire.

"What is it?" cried the Woodchucks. "Is it a bird? Is it a plane? No! It's a superhero!"

Doofus lifted the giant water tank, filled it with water from the lake, and flew over the woods, pouring water over the burning area. He put the fire out in no time.

"Now that's what I call a superhero!" said Huey.

"Superdoo always wins!" called Doofus, flying into the clouds.

"Thanks, Superdoo!" they all called out.

Meanwhile, Feox and Bobox were thinking up a new plan for getting back the crystal. They would bomb the reservoir, and flood the whole valley—including the camp.

"Remember," warned Feox. "We need half an hour to get clear."

"I know!" said Bobox, working on the timer. But the bomb exploded suddenly, and the two aliens were swept away by the flood.

"The reservoir's been hit! Take cover!" ordered Launchpad.
"Only Superdoo can save us now!" cried Dewey.

Superdoo flew overhead, carrying a mound of mud. He faced the flood, took a deep breath and blew until the water turned back. Then he patched up the reservoir with the mud, and it was good as new.

"Superdoo is great!" laughed Louie.

"You know," said Huey, "Doofus and Superdoo never seem to be around at the same time! Let's find out if it's just coincidence."

When Doofus went back to the hut to change, the brothers caught him. At last, he told them all about the crystal.

"So, that's how you beat us," frowned Louie. "Junior Woodchucks are supposed to be fair, Doofus!"

"I-I'm s-s-sorry," stammered Doofus. "I didn't mean to hurt anyone. Please listen."

But they walked off, disgusted.

"I used this stone for selfish reasons, and didn't realize my friends would be hurt," Doofus said to himself sadly. "I never want to see it again as long as I live!"

He tossed the stone away over his shoulder. It hit Feox on the head. Bobox picked it up.

"I don't understand any of this," he said, "but let's get out of here before anything else happens."

Soon Bobox and Feox were back in space, and Doofus had
returned to camp, where he found Launchpad and the boys
under attack by wolves.

"Run!" they yelled.

But Doofus, using all his courage, ran up to the platform
where the water tank stood and pushed against it with all his
might. The tank toppled from its perch and fell right on top of
the wolves, trapping them inside.

"Doofus, you're a hero!" cried Dewey. "And you did it all
without the crystal!"

That night, the boys sat around the campfire listening to a ghost story. They nearly jumped out of their skins when they heard a loud crash!

It was Doofus. He had tried to find his way back from the river in the dark, and ended up on the ground, with broken dishes everywhere.

Everyone gave a cheer for Doofus—the clumsiest hero ever!